Great
Irish Heroes

Written by
Fiona Waters

Illustrated by
Gilly Marklew

Gill & Macmillan

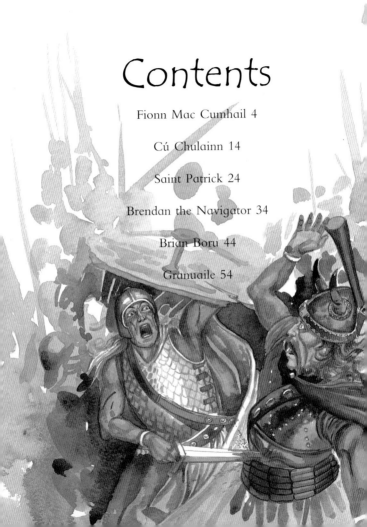

Contents

Fionn Mac Cumhail 4

Cú Chulainn 14

Saint Patrick 24

Brendan the Navigator 34

Brian Boru 44

Granuaile 54

Introduction

This collection of six exciting stories will
fire the imagination of readers, young and
old. Read the stirring story of Fionn Mac
Cumhail who became leader of the Fianna,
share the extraordinary saga of Brian Boru
who defeated the Vikings at the Battle of
Clontarf, and find out why Setanta came to
be called the Hound of Culann.

Fionn Mac Cumhail

Fionn was a son of the mighty warrior, Cumhail, leader of the Fianna, a special army that guarded the King in Ireland. Cumhail had been killed by enemies in a fierce battle just before Fionn was born. Cumhail's wife feared that these enemies might kill Fionn too, so she took the tiny baby on a dangerous journey to find Bodball, a druidess, and Fiacal, a female warrior.

"I have brought you Fionn, son of Cumhail," she shouted across the bog, to the rough cave where both women sheltered.
"I will leave him in your care so that no enemies can find him."

Bodball and Fiacal agreed to look after Fionn. "We will call him Demne and we will hide him away where none shall ever find him, not even yourself," they said. His mother loved Fionn dearly but she knew she had to make this sacrifice. She kissed her sleeping son on his forehead and turned away, blinded by tears.

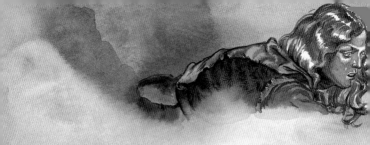

From then on, Fionn became Demne.
As he grew up, he learned how to
defend himself single-handed against an army
of men. He learned how to live wild on the
hillside, with only his wits and his spear to
find food. Bodball and Fiacal taught him to
make magic spells. But a warrior also needed
to learn the art of poetry, so they sent him to
study with the poet Finnéigeas.

Finnéigeas was an old man. He lived by the
River Boyne, near a deep pool. It was said
that a great fish – the Salmon of Knowledge
– lived in this pool and that the person who
caught it and ate it would know everything
there was to know in the world.

One day, Finnéigeas was fishing
in the pool, spear in hand.
Suddenly he gave a great shout.
"Demne! Demne! Come quickly. I have
finally caught the Salmon of Knowledge."

"Make a fire and cook the
fish for me," commanded Finnéigeas. "But
take great care that no flesh reaches your
mouth, for that prize is mine. I have waited
years for this moment."

Demne cooked the salmon carefully.
But as he was about to pass it to Finnéigeas,
the cooked flesh loosened and the fish slipped
down the stick. Demne put out his hand to
steady it, but it was very hot and it burned
his thumb. Without thinking, he thrust the
thumb into his mouth!

Finnéigeas cried out, and looked deep into
Demne's eyes. "What is your real name,
Demne?" he asked the astonished young
man. "My mother called me Fionn, son of
Cumhail," he replied. "Why do you ask?"
"There is no more I can teach you, Fionn.
You must eat the whole salmon now, then
go to take your place at the head of the
King's great army. You will be leader
of the Fianna."

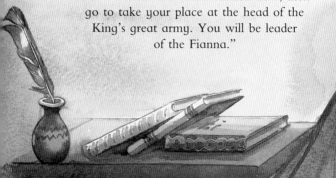

From that time on, Fionn possessed
a wealth of knowledge. Whenever he
needed to know something, he had
only to place his thumb in his
mouth – and all was revealed!

Fionn said goodbye to Finnéigeas and set off to join the King and the Fianna. It was the festival of Samhain, and the King was holding a great feast at Tara. Powerful warriors and chieftains gathered at court for the celebrations. The huge hall at Tara was overflowing and mighty fires crackled. Servants ran in with huge platters of wild boar and all kinds of roasted meats. Wine flowed from jugs, laughter filled the air and dogs scurried under tables looking for scraps.

Silence fell in the great hall as Fionn burst through the doors. "Who are you that dares to march in here so boldly?" asked the King. "I am Fionn, son of Cumhail," answered Fionn proudly. "You are welcome here, Fionn, son of the man who was a great friend to me," the King said. "How may I serve you, my King?" Fionn asked.

Then the King told Fionn a strange story. Every Samhain, Tara was besieged by an evil spirit which appeared in the shape of a fire-breathing dragon. This dragon played sweet music; anyone who heard it fell into a deep sleep. Many warriors had tried to slay the dragon but all had died in the attempt. Many magicians too had used spells to destroy the dragon, but they had failed also.

"I will slay this dragon for you, my King," vowed Fionn, and he strode out into the dark night to wait for it. A gentle voice spoke to him. "Fionn, your father was a good friend to me." Fionn looked round but he could see no one in the velvet blackness.

"You will not see me," said the voice, "but look up, and you will see a spear." And there, above Fionn's head hung a finely decorated silver spear. "When the dragon begins to play music," said the voice, "place the spear against your forehead. The spells will become useless."

At last he heard it, a single note played on a pipe with almost enchanting sweetness. But remembering, he pressed the sword to his forehead and the music stopped. There before him stood the dragon! He hurled the spear straight between its eyes and it fell instantly to the ground! With one swing, Fionn cut off its head and brought it to the King, bowing before him.

And that is how Fionn Mac Cumhail became the greatest leader of the Fianna.

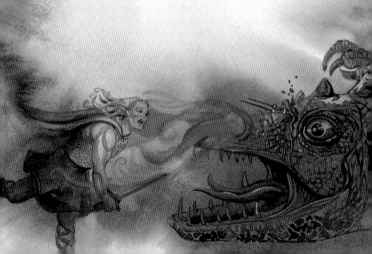

Cú Chulainn

Setanta sat on the wall, kicking his heels. He was restless and he was cross. Although still only a young boy, he wanted to become a warrior. He dreamt of joining the Red Branch Knights who fought for his uncle, the King of Ulster, Conchobar Mac Nessa. But his mother, Dechtire, was worried about his safety.

"You must wait until you are older," said Dechtire to her son. "There is no place for a young boy in the rough and tumble of the King's court at Emain Macha!" But Setanta wouldn't be put off. He felt sure that if only he could take part in the special game of hurling that was played there, the King would notice him and mark him out for a warrior in the future.

Setanta made up his mind.

He waited until his mother was busy preparing supper, jumped off the wall and snatched up his hurley stick and ball. He set off in the direction of Emain Macha. It was a long and dangerous journey but Setanta's determination drove him onwards.

As he approached the court, he saw to his delight that a hurling match was in progress. He ran straight onto the field and was soon in the thick of the game. The other boys were almost fully grown compared to himself. Setanta avoided all their tackles and, whirling past them, sent a long, low ball – straight into the goal!

There was a huge roar of anger.
Not only had Setanta appeared as if from
nowhere, he hadn't even asked permission to
join their game. The players descended on
him, brandishing their sticks, shouting and
yelling with rage.

Inside, the noise reached Conchobar who
thought he was being attacked. He ran out
with his warriors to defend Emain Macha.
Once he saw what was going on, he
bellowed at the older boys to be silent, and
looked in astonishment at the young and
very fierce-looking boy who was the cause of
all the commotion.

"Who are you and why are you here, bold,
wild lad?" he demanded of Setanta.

Not in the least frightened, Setanta shouted back, "I am your nephew, Setanta, proud son of your sister, Dechtire, and I am going to be one of your warriors!"

Conchobar flung back his head with a huge laugh. "Well, young warrior, you certainly don't lack courage, even if your manners are not of the best. You shall indeed stay here and be one of my warriors if that is truly what you want."

That is how Setanta came to Emain Macha and began his training for the Red Branch Knights. It was hard work. Not only did he learn to fight, but he also learnt how to track as silently as a shadow, and to move with all the cunning of the grey wolves. He learnt discipline and honour, and he even learnt some manners. He grew to be greatly respected by his fellows.

One day Conchobar was invited to a feast given by Culann the Smith. The King looked around for Setanta to ride by his side. As usual, Setanta was playing hurling, beating a great troop of other warriors single-handed. Laughing, Conchobar bid Setanta ride after him once the game was finished, to join in the feasting.

But when Conchobar arrived at Culann's house, he soon forgot Setanta, as the wine flowed and the delicious smell of roasting meats filled the hall. Time passed and the evening grew dark, the heavy rain lashed against the huge oak doors, and the wind sent the smoke from the great log fire tumbling back down the chimney.

Culann called his guards into the shelter of the hall saying, "I have a mighty hound who will watch the door and protect us from all danger. Only a fool would be out on a night like this!" Still Conchobar did not remember Setanta.

Much later that night, as the firelight
flickered on the rough stone walls, there
was suddenly a terrible commotion outside.
The deep-throated baying of the hound,
mingled with vicious snarls,
woke Conchobar with a start.

"Setanta!" he cried in horror, "I have
forgotten Setanta! He will be torn to
shreds." He leapt to his feet, running
towards the doors. But the doors
burst inwards. There was a flurry
of rain and wind and a figure
swept inside, kicking the door
shut behind him. It was Setanta!

Culann looked at him in amazement. "Where is my hound? How did you get past him?" Then everyone in the hall saw that the mighty dog was slung over Setanta's shoulders, and that it was dead. With only his hurley stick and ball in his hand to defend himself, Setanta had killed it. Culann was mightily relieved that Setanta was alive and well, but he mourned the loss of his brave and faithful hound. Setanta laid the dead dog at his feet.

"From henceforth, I shall be your hound. I will guard your house with my life," he pledged. And that is how Setanta came to be called Cú Chulainn, the Hound of Culann.

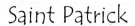

Saint Patrick

Patrick stood on the deck of a boat as it rolled up and down in the swell of the sea. He peered into the misty distance and caught sight of the shore. Patrick was returning to Ireland, the country where he had been sent as a slave when he was 16 years old.

He had escaped from harsh slavery as a young man and, after many travels and adventures, had settled in France where he became a priest. There he had a dream, telling him to return to Ireland and take God's message to the people.

Now Patrick watched as the sailors skilfully guided the boat in between jagged rocks, and in a moment he heard the scrape of pebbles against the bottom of the boat. He pulled his rough woollen robes up around his waist and jumped ashore. The sailors called goodbye and turned the tiny boat around once more, out to sea. Patrick stood on the beach. His mission to convert the pagan Druid people of Ireland to Christianity was about to begin.

In time, Patrick heard that Laoghaire, the High King of Tara, had summoned all the chiefs of Ireland to a great feast. The Druids were about to celebrate the coming of spring with a special ceremony. The High King commanded that all fires and lights in his household, and in all the surrounding lands, were to be put out until a great fire was lit on the royal Hill of Tara.

This pagan festival was to take place at the same time as the Christian celebration of Easter. Patrick decided to show the pagan people the power of Christianity. He and a small group of followers walked to the Hill of Slane, which was at the opposite end of the valley to the Hill of Tara. There they lit their own huge fire and watched it blaze high into the sky.

The Druids were very angry when they saw this. They thought Patrick wished to be stronger than the High King of Tara. They told the King that if he was to keep his power over the people, he must defeat Patrick. So they ordered their fire on the Hill of Tara to be lit and soon the whole valley was aglow from the fires at each end. It was a spectacular sight that men would talk about for many years to come.

Then the King and the Druids and a great band of soldiers marched across the valley towards Slane. They tried very hard to put out Patrick's huge fire but all their efforts failed. They even tried to kill Patrick but he stood bravely in front of the fire, singing hymns and praising God. And so the fire burned through the night and its light shone the length and breadth of the land. The King realised Patrick was not going to be defeated by force, and it made him thoughtful. Perhaps, after all, the Druids did not have all the answers.

The next day, King Laoghaire asked
Patrick to come to Tara and tell him
about Christianity.

On the way, Patrick picked a bunch of
shamrock, a plant that was sacred to the
Druids; he tucked it into his robes.

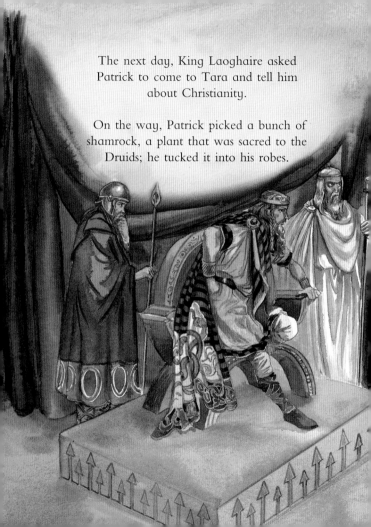

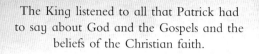

The King listened to all that Patrick had
to say about God and the Gospels and the
beliefs of the Christian faith.

Some of it was very difficult for the King to
understand, especially the Christian belief in
the Trinity: how could God actually be
three people, the Father,
the Son and the Holy Ghost?

Suddenly Patrick had an idea.
He pulled out the bunch of
shamrock and broke off one
leaf. There were the three
petals on the one stem, three
in one – just like the Trinity!

The King understood Christianity that day and realised that Patrick did not want to be more powerful than him. He gave Patrick permission to preach the Gospel throughout the land. And so it was that Patrick came back to Ireland in peace and with the message of God. Eventually he became the patron saint of Ireland, and the shamrock became the national emblem.

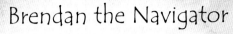

Brendan the Navigator

Brendan straightened up with a groan. His back was aching from leaning over his boat as he prepared for a very special voyage. Not for nothing was Brendan called 'The Navigator', but this latest adventure was his bravest yet. Brendan was planning to travel to the 'Promised Land of the Saints'. It was not certain that this land was real, but Brendan was determined to look for it.

The journey would be long and dangerous and Brendan was already an old man. In fact he was nearly 85 so it was small wonder that his back ached! Most of his fellow monks considered him mad. Now he went slowly into the shelter of the monastery and joined the rest of the monks for what was to be his last meal on dry land – for a very long time indeed!

The following morning dawned clear and
cold: ideal sailing conditions. After a simple
meal of porridge, Brendan and his crew
walked to the shore, and, with a blessing
from the Abbot, launched the currach. It
seemed a frail craft for such a long voyage
ahead, but Brendan smiled confidently as
he took his place on board. As they sailed
away, he watched the coastline of Ireland
grow smaller and smaller. At last all he
could see around was the great empty sea.

For many days no land
was sighted; food and water became
short. Brendan and the monks sometimes
caught fish but they were relieved when they
finally saw land, far away on the horizon.
As they drew nearer, they saw an island,
covered in hundreds of sheep. Brendan kept a
diary of his voyage and, that night, when he
wrote his usual report, he called the place the
Island of Sheep, the Faroe Islands.

Next morning Brendan decided they should
light a fire and celebrate Mass. They found a
great hill by the shore, overlooking the island
and the sea, and Brendan asked the younger
monks to build a fire there. As it burned
merrily, Brendan prepared
for the service.

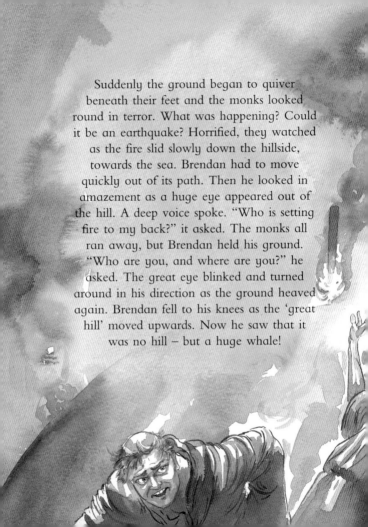

Suddenly the ground began to quiver beneath their feet and the monks looked round in terror. What was happening? Could it be an earthquake? Horrified, they watched as the fire slid slowly down the hillside, towards the sea. Brendan had to move quickly out of its path. Then he looked in amazement as a huge eye appeared out of the hill. A deep voice spoke. "Who is setting fire to my back?" it asked. The monks all ran away, but Brendan held his ground. "Who are you, and where are you?" he asked. The great eye blinked and turned around in his direction as the ground heaved again. Brendan fell to his knees as the 'great hill' moved upwards. Now he saw that it was no hill – but a huge whale!

"My name is Jasconius. As you see,
I am a whale," said the deep voice again.

And truly there it was. A great whale
who had been peacefully sleeping by the
shore, half in and half out of the water.
Brendan struggled to pour water over the
huge creature's back where the fire had been
lit. The whale's body shook, and Brendan
suddenly realised that the creature was
laughing at him.

"Gentle monk, do not fear. You have not
hurt me, but the warmth of your fire has
woken me up."

The monks were a little ashamed as they crept back to see what had become of Brendan. They were astonished to find him sitting on the sand, calmly talking to the mighty whale.

"My friends, you have no cause to be frightened," he called to them. "See here, this noble creature has offered to pass messages to all his brethren so that we may travel safely over the seas between here and the Promised Land."

And Jasconius was as good as his word. For the rest of their voyage, whenever Brendan and his monks met any whales, all of whom would play and leap around their boat, the creatures were careful to do them no harm and to point out the safest passage.

Finally, they arrived at a beautiful island
which Brendan felt sure was, at last, the
'Promised Land of the Saints'. He was
utterly weary from the difficulties and
adventures of their travels but his heart
almost burst with joy.

"My brethren, we have reached our
destination! This is the Promised Land! Let us
give our thanks to God!" He led the monks
in happy prayers and joyful singing.

The journey had taken seven years. Some people believe that the Promised Land was America, although it was a further nine centuries before another man made a similar voyage. His name was Christopher Columbus.

Brian Boru

Brian shifted in his saddle. The Vikings were fighting the people of Ireland and Brian had spent many hours in battle. He was utterly weary but he was determined not to show it. He was a warrior, from the tribe of Dal Cais, and a son of Cennetig who had once been King of Munster. Brian was still a boy, with a short spear in his grubby hand. His older brother, Mahon, had succeeded Cennetig as King. But in his heart, Brian held a secret: Eimer the fortune-teller had told him that one day he would be Ireland's greatest King.

The cries of battle chilled his blood and, as Brian looked round, he saw the Viking charge approach. He gripped his spear tightly and looked for Mahon who was in the thick of the fighting. But this time the Vikings were too strong and the Dal Cais were forced back, even to the gates of their fort.

Brian watched in mounting horror as these
wild Norsemen ran through the settlement.

Next day a deep sadness hung over the ruined houses. Brian's own mother had been killed in the raid. Brian went to Mahon and, clasping his spear, spoke, his voice at first shaky but then gradually stronger: "I pledge today that I will avenge the death of my mother and will not rest until these Norsemen have been driven from Ireland for ever!"

Mahon saw the cold rage in his brother's eyes and realised that, although he was still a boy, he had grown up that day. "Bravely spoken, my brother! We will fight side by side, and I will be proud to have you with me," he cried.

The years passed with many more fierce battles. Brian grew to be taller and stronger than Mahon. And he grew braver too. One day, Mahon proposed a treaty with the Vikings. "They are too strong for us, we cannot have any more of our countrymen killed," he declared.

But Brian still remembered how the Vikings had killed their mother. He would never bow to the Norsemen. So he broke away from his brother and many followed him, for he was skilled in warfare and tactics. Brian waited for the chance to fight the Vikings.

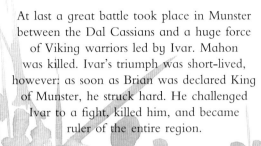

At last a great battle took place in Munster
between the Dal Cassians and a huge force
of Viking warriors led by Ivar. Mahon
was killed. Ivar's triumph was short-lived,
however: as soon as Brian was declared King
of Munster, he struck hard. He challenged
Ivar to a fight, killed him, and became
ruler of the entire region.

By now, he was ruler of almost the whole of Ireland, except for one man: Malachy, King of Meath. The two men were both proud and stubborn and neither would give in at first, but finally Malachy agreed to support Brian. It was the year 1002 and Brian was at last acknowledged as High King of all Ireland – just as Eimer had predicted.

He was called Brian Borumha,
Brian of the Tributes.

Brian aimed to restore peace and prosperity to the land after many years of desperate warfare. He ruled his warriors with a firm hand so that farmers could once more return to the land and school-teachers to their classrooms. He rebuilt many of the churches that the Vikings had destroyed. He travelled round the country in a fine cavalcade so that everyone might see him and give him due homage.

Brian Boru grew to be an old man. Perhaps he ruled with too strong a hand. Some of his people became unhappy and resentful. Maelmordha, King of Leinster, decided to challenge him. He sent messengers to the Vikings and to Iceland, asking for support, and in time he amassed a huge army to challenge Brian.

The Battle of Clontarf was the fiercest in all Irish history. It began on the morning of Good Friday, 23 April, in the year 1014. Back and forth the opposing forces fought, gaining here, losing there. Brian was convinced that he would win, and so it was. The Vikings were finally driven back into the sea.

Brian stayed awhile on the battlefield with only one servant; there he prayed, giving thanks for yet another successful encounter. But, unknown to him, there was still a small band of Norse warriors determined to end his rule once and for all. If they couldn't have Ireland, they would at least get rid of its troublesome king. A warrior, Brodir, from the Isle of Man, struck the fatal blow! Within hours of winning the greatest battle of his long reign, Brian lay dead.

His heartbroken warriors held a huge 'wake' that lasted for twelve days and twelve nights. Bards sang of his exploits; storytellers recounted his deeds of huge courage. His body was taken in great state to Armagh where he was finally laid to rest.

Brian Boru was the greatest warrior Ireland has ever seen.

Granuaile

Granuaile was the daughter of the chieftain Owen Dubhdara. She grew up in Belclare Castle, a fortified tower with a great hall where the clans would gather for huge feasts. She had been christened Grainne. From early childhood, she loved being with her father on board one of his great fleet of ships. Her father did his best to discourage her because she was a girl, but Grainne was determined. She cut off all her hair off and borrowed some of her brother's clothes. When she appeared dressed as a boy and demanding to be taken on the next voyage, her mother was angry, but her father laughingly agreed to take her with him. And so her life on the high seas began. From then on she was known as Grainne Mhaol, Bald Grace, and in time this name became shortened to Granuaile.

In those days, girls got married very young, and Granuaile's husband was called Donal O'Flaherty. Her parents thought he might be able to tame their wild daughter, because he was known as Donal an Chogaidh, 'Donal of the Battles'. But although she bore three children, she became more and more involved in the adventures of the O'Flaherty clan. She had learnt much at her father's side and men were impressed with her skill and her success. When Donal was killed in an ambush, Granuaile defended her castle successfully against her husband's enemies.

Although the O'Flahertys admired Granuaile greatly, they were not prepared to accept her as their leader after Donal was killed. So Granuaile returned to her father who was very proud of his daughter's exploits. He gave her the castle on Clare Island to live in and there she set up as a chieftain in her own right, with some two hundred followers. Granuaile then turned to piracy and soon became the most daring and most feared pirate on the west coast, her coffers overflowing with stolen treasure.

By now the English realised that she was making it too dangerous for them to travel by sea and that she had to be stopped. She finally met her match in the new governor of Connaught, Sir Richard Bingham. He chased her on the seas, threatened to put her to death and finally imprisoned her. Two years in Dublin Castle almost destroyed her brave spirit, but she was released when she promised to give up piracy.

By now Granuaile was growing old and she
decided to write to Elizabeth I,
Queen of England, to ask for the Queen's
protection in the future. In time the Queen
replied, asking several questions. Granuaile
decided to travel to London to see her.

As she waited to be received by the Queen,
she began to daydream about the exciting
life she had led and did not hear the
Queen's servant speak.

"Madam!" he said. "I insist you accompany me to the inner chamber. Her Gracious Majesty Queen Elizabeth is ready to receive you." Granuaile started back from her daydreaming. She looked down her haughty nose at the impatient courtier. "Do not sneer at me, you popinjay," she roared. "Do not believe that I am not an important person just because I do not wear fine clothes like the Queen of England. In my lands I am as powerful as your Gracious Queen."

Granuaile brushed the courtier aside, and strode off to meet the Queen.

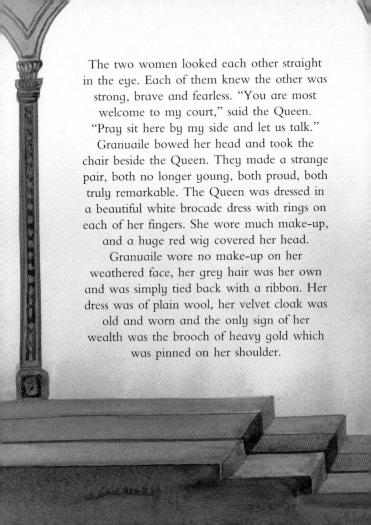

The two women looked each other straight in the eye. Each of them knew the other was strong, brave and fearless. "You are most welcome to my court," said the Queen. "Pray sit here by my side and let us talk." Granuaile bowed her head and took the chair beside the Queen. They made a strange pair, both no longer young, both proud, both truly remarkable. The Queen was dressed in a beautiful white brocade dress with rings on each of her fingers. She wore much make-up, and a huge red wig covered her head. Granuaile wore no make-up on her weathered face, her grey hair was her own and was simply tied back with a ribbon. Her dress was of plain wool, her velvet cloak was old and worn and the only sign of her wealth was the brooch of heavy gold which was pinned on her shoulder.

The two women talked for a long
time, to the amazement of the rest of the
courtiers. And when Granuaile walked out
of the court that day, she held her head even
higher. The Queen had granted every one
of Granuaile's requests. Her brother and
her son were released from prison, and she
herself was provided with a living
for the rest of her days.

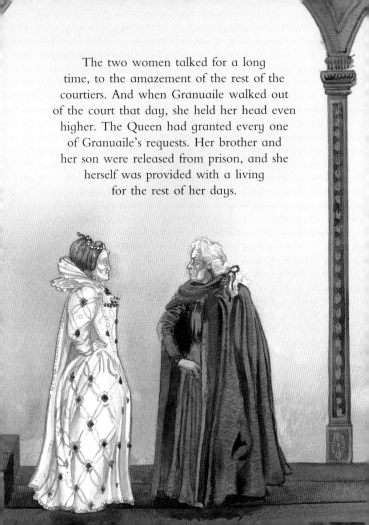

Granuaile lived until she was in her seventies, a good age for those times. Even as an old woman, she remained a leader who was admired by all her followers. And by a strange coincidence, she died in 1603, the same year as Queen Elizabeth – two women who, despite their very different lives, had met and understood each other.

For Dáire McMillen, with love

Illustrated by Gilly Marklew
Edited by Deirdre Rennison Kunz
and Sheila Mortimer
Designed by Juliet Turner

Published by Gill & Macmillan Ltd
Hume Avenue, Park West, Dublin 12
with associated companies throughout the world
www.gillmacmillan.ie

ISBN 978 07171 4219 4

This edition produced by
Tony Potter Publishing Ltd, RH17 5PA
Copyright © 2007 Tony Potter Publishing Ltd
www.tonypotter.com

Printed in China
3 5 7 9 10 8 6 4